GULLIVER'S TRAVELS
IN LILLIPUT

JONATHAN SWIFT

Retold by
ANGELA WILKES

Illustrated by
PETER DENNIS

Series editor: Heather Amery

Many years ago there lived in England a man called Lemuel Gulliver. He loved travelling and had already sailed all round the world.

One day he boarded a ship bound for the Far East, little knowing that this was to be the strangest adventure of his life.

The voyage began well, but as the ship approached the East Indies a mighty storm blew the ship a long way off course.

Soon there was no fresh food or water left and some of the sailors caught a fever. Gulliver tried to look after them but many men died.

One night there was another fierce storm. Strong winds and rough seas drove the ship on to sharp rocks and wrecked it.

Gulliver swam for his life, hoping there was land nearby. At last, just as he was giving up hope, he felt ground beneath his feet.

He stumbled ashore and fell down on a grassy slope. The grass was short and very soft and he was so tired, he was soon fast asleep.

Some of the crew tried to escape in a rowing boat, but it overturned in the huge waves and everyone drowned except for Gulliver.

When Gulliver finally awoke after a long, deep sleep, he tried to stand up. To his surprise, he found that he could not move.

His arms and legs were tied to the ground and his hair was pinned down. He could not even turn his head away from the glare of the sun.

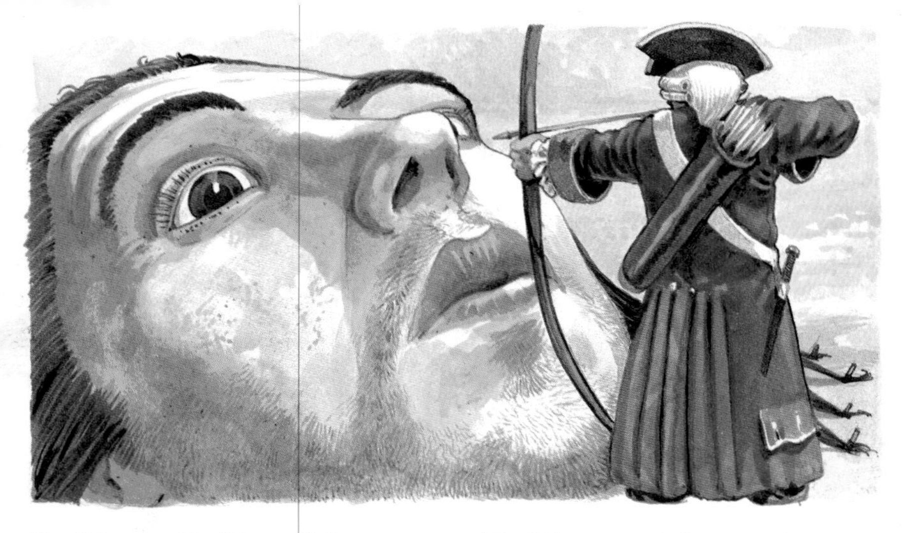

Suddenly Gulliver felt some thing small and light move up his body and stop just below his chin. He peered downwards as best he could.

To his astonishment he saw a tiny man, only about six inches tall, standing on his chest and pointing a bow and arrow at his nose.

Then about forty more little men scrambled up on to Gulliver's chest. None of them was bigger than his hand and they were all armed.

Gulliver was so surprised, he shouted loudly. The noise was deafening to the little men and they all fell over or ran away in fright.

But soon their courage returned and they came back again. One brave man crept right up to Gulliver's face. "Hekina degul!" he cried in a shrill voice, staring at Gulliver in amazement.

Gulliver struggled to get free. He managed to break some of the strings tying him and to free one arm. Then he pulled out the pegs holding down his hair so he could turn his head.

But when he tried to sit up hundreds of tiny men all round him shouted and fired arrows at him. These pricked Gulliver's face and hands painfully, like thousands of tiny needles.

Other men jabbed at Gulliver's sides with spears but luckily the spears did not pierce his leather jerkin. "I had better lie still and see what happens," thought Gulliver.

After a while the men stopped firing arrows and Gulliver heard a knocking sound. He turned his head to see what was happening.

The little men were building a platform near him. It was eighteen inches high and big enough to hold four of the tiny people.

An important looking man went up on to the platform and made a long speech in a strange language. Gulliver did not understand a word.

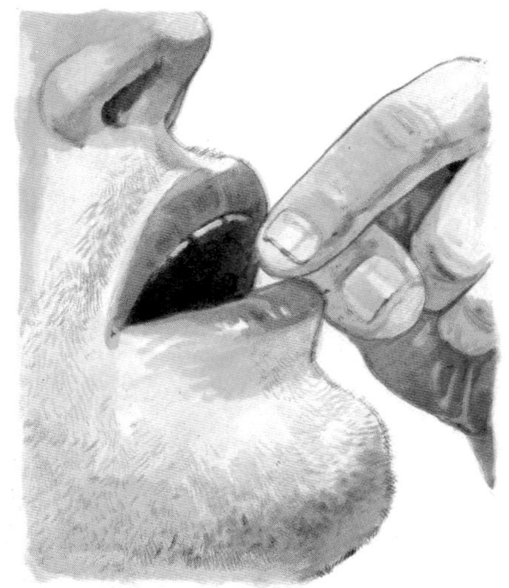

He spoke back and tried to show that he was hungry by putting a finger to his mouth. He had not eaten since before the shipwreck.

The man understood. He shouted orders and the tiny people propped ladders against Gulliver. They climbed up them and walked towards Gulliver's mouth, carrying baskets of food.

In the baskets there were small joints of meat, and loaves of bread the size of buttons. Gulliver ate two of everything at a time. The tiny people were amazed at how much he could eat.

Then Gulliver showed them he was thirsty and they brought him barrels and barrels of wine. He drank each barrel in one swig.

The people were so delighted by this that they danced on Gulliver's chest. He was surprised they were no longer frightened of him.

When he had finished his meal a nobleman from the Court walked up to his face and waved a message at him. It was from the Emperor.

He made a speech and then left. Gulliver soon fell into a deep sleep. He did not know there had been a sleeping drug in his wine.

While Gulliver slept, five hundred carpenters built a giant trolley next to him, hoisted him on to it and harnessed it to 1,500 horses.

They set off towards Mildendo, the capital city of the land. The emperor had ordered that Gulliver be taken there.

The journey took over a day and the procession finally stopped in front of a grand temple not far from the city. The temple was to be Gulliver's home, as it was the largest building in the land. It was just big enough for Gulliver to lie down in.

The emperor came to look at Gulliver. He watched from the top of a nearby tower as Gulliver was chained to the temple.

Once Gulliver's chains were secure, his ropes were cut and he could stand up. The crowd gasped in wonder as he rose to his feet.

Towering above the crowds, Gulliver had a bird's eye view of the countryside around him. Everything was tiny. "It looks like a miniature garden," thought Gulliver. The tallest trees were only about three feet high and the fields seemed no larger than people's flowerbeds in England. The city not far away looked like a brightly coloured model village.

The emperor came down from the tower and ordered his servants to give Gulliver more food and drink that was ready for him. It was piled into little carts and the servants pushed them forwards to a place where Gulliver could bend down and reach them easily.

He picked up one cart and emptied it in two gulps, then he picked up another. Altogether he ate twenty whole cartloads of food.

When Gulliver had finished eating, the emperor went forwards to talk to him. He held his sword drawn, in case Gulliver attacked him.

Gulliver lay on his side so he and the emperor could talk to each other, but neither of them understood a word the other was saying.

Gulliver tried many languages, but the emperor did not understand any of them. He went away, leaving guards to protect Gulliver.

Everyone wanted to see the giant man. They pushed closer and closer and some men dodged past the guards and fired arrows at Gulliver.

The guards seized six of the ruffians and pushed them towards Gulliver to be punished. The men struggled and howled with fright.

Gulliver picked them up. He put five in his pocket and lifted the sixth to his mouth, as if he were about to eat him alive. The little man screamed and screamed, especially when Gulliver took out his penknife. But Gulliver just cut the ropes round his hands and gently put him down on the ground. He did the same with the rest of the ruffians and they all ran away.

As the days passed, thousands of people flocked to look at Gulliver. So many people went to see him that the emperor was worried no work was being done. He ordered that no one was allowed to visit Gulliver a second time unless they paid a lot of money.

He held meetings with his nobles to decide what to do with Gulliver. They thought he might be dangerous and that they ought to kill him.

Then two of Gulliver's guards went to one of the meetings and told how kind he had been to the rough people in the crowd.

This pleased the emperor and he ordered all the villages around Mildendo to supply enough food for Gulliver every day.

Then he gave Gulliver six hundred servants of his own. They lived in tents on either side of the entrance to Gulliver's temple home.

Three hundred tailors measured Gulliver for clothes and six clever men were sent to teach him their strange language.

Gulliver learnt the new language quickly and within three weeks he was able to talk to the emperor. "Please set me free," he begged. "You must wait for a while," the emperor replied. From then on Gulliver went to him every day and asked him again.

Then one day the emperor sent two officers to search Gulliver for dangerous weapons. They wanted to look in Gulliver's pockets, so he picked them up and put them into each of his pockets in turn. The officers made a long list of everything they found.

When they had finished their search, the two officers went to the emperor and read their list out loud to him.

"In the Man Mountain's right coat pocket we found a sheet of cloth big enough to be a carpet." This was Gulliver's handkerchief.

"In the left pocket there was a silver chest full of strange powder which made us sneeze." This was Gulliver's snuff box.

"In another pocket were sheets of paper bound together. They were covered with black marks which must have been writing."

"In a waistcoat pocket was a thing with poles sticking out from it. We think that the Man Mountain combs his head with this machine."

"In another pocket was an iron tube longer than a man. It had a wooden handle and bits of iron on it. We have no idea what this was."

"In one of the top pockets there was a round thing on a chain. It made a ticking noise and the Man Mountain kept looking at it."

"In another pocket he had a net full of gold coins. He said this was his purse. This was all we found in the Man Mountain's pockets."

When he had heard the list the emperor ordered his troops to surround Gulliver and told him to draw his scimitar. Gulliver waved it in the air and everyone gasped in fear.

Next he had to pull out the strange iron tube. Gulliver fired his pistol into the air and hundreds of soldiers fell down with fright. Then Gulliver handed his weapons to the emperor's guards.

As time went by Gulliver learnt that the island he was on was called Lilliput. He tried to please its tiny people, hoping one day they would free him. They soon grew to trust him. Even the children were not scared of him and played hide and seek in his hair.

One day Gulliver watched a strange competition. The men of Lilliput did tricks on a tightrope to win posts at the emperor's court.

Whoever was best won the best job. Flimnap had won his job as treasurer by making the rope higher and doing double somersaults.

There was another competition, called Leaping and Creeping. The emperor and one of his ministers held out a stick and the competitors had to leap over it or creep under it. The best people won coloured ribbons to tie round their waists.

One day Gulliver decided he would entertain the emperor. He made a platform out of a handkerchief tied tightly over some sticks.

He lifted some of the emperor's cavalry on to the platform and they staged a mock battle. The emperor was delighted with the show.

He persuaded the empress to let Gulliver hold her level with the platform so that she could have a good view of the performance.

During the show a messenger arrived. He told the emperor that some shepherds had found a large, strange object in a field.

He described the object and Gulliver realised that it was his hat, which he had lost. The next day the shepherds brought it to him.

It was very dusty because it had been dragged along the ground all the way to the city, but Gulliver was pleased to have it back.

At last the emperor set Gulliver free. He could go where he liked as long as he asked permission and stayed on the main roads. The emperor told him he could go into the city.

Everyone was warned Gulliver was coming. They stayed indoors so they would not be trodden on and watched from their windows as Gulliver stepped carefully through the streets.

Gulliver wanted to visit the palace, but the gate was too small for him to go through and the walls too high for him to step over.

Then he had an idea. He went to the Royal Park and cut down some trees with his penknife. With the wood from these he made two stools.

He took them back to the palace and put one on each side of the wall. Then he used them as stepping stones to climb over the wall.

He lay down and looked through the windows of the palace into the royal apartments. The windows had been left open for him.

It was like looking into a doll's house. The rooms were furnished with tiny tables and chairs to fit the tiny people who used them.

The empress was sitting by one of the palace windows with her children. They were all waiting to see the Man Mountain.

The empress smiled when she saw Gulliver. "Welcome," she said and she held out her hand so that Gulliver could kiss it.

One morning, soon after Gulliver's visit to the palace, Reldresaal, the emperor's secretary, paid him a visit.

"There are problems at court," he told Gulliver. "There are two rival groups of men trying to win power in the land."

"One group, the Tramecksans, wears high heels and the other, the Slamecksans, low heels. Neither group will speak to the other."

"The emperor likes low heels, so at the moment the Slamecksans have more power. But a civil war could break out at any time."

"As well as these problems," Reldresaal went on, "we are at war with a neighbouring island called Blefescu where the people are no bigger than us. You might think the war rather strange. We are fighting over which is the right end to start eating a boiled egg.

We always used to break our eggs at the big end, but many years ago one of the princes cut his finger as he broke open his egg.

His father, the emperor of Lilliput, at once ordered that from then on everyone had to break open their eggs at the smaller end.

But many people refused to do this. Thousands preferred to die rather than give in to the new law and break their eggs at the small end.

The people of Blefescu still broke their eggs at the big end, so many of the rebels from Lilliput fled to Blefescu and lived there.

The two kingdoms have been at war for years and many people have been killed. Now Blefescu's fleet is preparing to invade us."

"The emperor needs your help if he is to win this war," said Reldresaal. "I will do what I can," Gulliver promised him.

Gulliver decided to look at Blefescu. He walked to the coast of Lilliput and lay down behind a small hill to spy on the other island.

He took out his telescope so he could study the enemy fleet more closely. There were about fifty warships and some smaller ones.

Gulliver returned home and asked for ropes and iron bars. He twisted the ropes together to make them strong and bent the bars into hooks.

Then he went back to the coast and waded into the sea, carrying the ropes and hooks. He headed towards Blefescu's fleet.

Gulliver had to swim across the middle part of the channel between Lilliput and Blefescu, as the sea was deep. As only his head was above water, the enemy did not see him until he was very close. They screamed with fright and jumped overboard to escape.

Gulliver fastened ropes to the ships and cut their anchors loose. The people of Blefescu fired thousands of arrows at him.

Gulliver put on his glasses so he could carry on with his work. The tiny arrows stuck in his face and hands but his eyes were safe.

He tied all the ropes together and headed back for Lilliput, pulling the ships behind him. The enemy shouted with rage when they saw their entire fleet being towed away.

As Gulliver approached the shore of Lilliput he saw the emperor and the court waiting for him. "Long live the emperor!" he cried and everyone welcomed him home with shouts and cheers.

The emperor was not satisfied for long with Gulliver capturing the fleet. "You must help me conquer Blefescu," he told him.

"I won't make free people into slaves," said Gulliver. The emperor was annoyed. After this he was no longer very friendly to Gulliver.

Three weeks later six ambassadors came from Blefescu to make peace with Lilliput. Gulliver met them while they were there and they invited him to visit Blefescu later on. The emperor of Lilliput gave him permission to go, but he looked very angry.

A few days after the ambassadors had left Gulliver was able to do the emperor a service. Late one night he was woken up by shouting outside his temple.

"Come quickly," a voice cried. "The empress's palace is on fire." Gulliver ran to the palace, trying not to step on the tiny people rushing around everywhere.

There was chaos at the palace. The little people were passing buckets of water along to the fire, but the buckets were only the size of thimbles and the flames roared as fiercely as ever. Gulliver helped and within minutes he had put out the fire. The palace was saved and he went back home to bed.

Gulliver was happy living in Lilliput and had every thing he needed. Two hundred needlewomen made shirts for him.

Their cloth was so fine that they had to quilt layers of it together to make it thick and strong enough for Gulliver to wear.

To find out Gulliver's size, the women measured round his thumb. They said they could work out the rest of his measurements from this.

Three hundred tailors made a new suit for Gulliver. They measured him by dropping a plumb line from his neck to the ground.

When Gulliver's suit was finished, it fitted well, but it looked as if it was made of patchwork all the same colour.

Three hundred chefs cooked Gulliver's food every day and 120 waiters served it to him, hoisting it on to the table with pulleys.

The emperor was curious to see how Gulliver lived. One evening he and his family went to have dinner with Gulliver at his home.

Gulliver picked them up and put them on the table in front of him. They had a magnificent feast and enjoyed themselves.

Flimnap, the treasurer, was also there. He did not like Gulliver and kept glaring at him, but Gulliver took no notice and went on eating.

Flimnap was annoyed and whispered to the emperor, complaining about how much it cost to feed Gulliver. The emperor looked cross.

Late one night, as Gulliver was planning his visit to Blefescu, he had a surprise visit from one of the highest nobles of the court.

He told Gulliver to send his servants away, then spoke to him secretly. "Your life is in great danger," he said.

"You have enemies at court. Flimnap and the admiral have accused you of being a traitor and have written out a list of your crimes."

They say you have been plotting against the emperor with the people of Blefescu and that you should be punished by death.

Flimnap suggested that your temple be set on fire and that you be shot with poisoned arrows as you try to escape from the blaze.

But Reldresaal reminded the court of how useful you had been. He suggested it might be kinder to spare your life and just make you blind.

The emperor agreed to this but thought you should also be slowly starved, to save money. The court praised him for his great generosity."

Gulliver knew he had to act quickly. He wrote to the emperor, saying he was leaving at once for his promised visit to Blefescu.

He did not wait for an answer to his letter but set off straightaway for the coast. He stole one of the largest ships in the Lilliputian fleet and tied a rope to its prow.

He took off his clothes, bundled them up and put them on the ship. Then, pulling the ship along behind him, he waded out to sea and swam across the channel to Blefescu.

When Gulliver reached Blefescu, he went to the capital city. The king came out to meet him and Gulliver lay down to kiss his hand. The king was not at all scared and welcomed Gulliver warmly, saying he could stay in Blefescu for as long as he liked.

A few days later Gulliver saw something odd out at sea. It was a full-sized boat which had overturned! Gulliver was very excited.

He rushed back to the king. “Please help me to get this boat,” he begged him. “It may be my only chance to return home.”

The king lent him twenty big ships and three thousand sailors. They sailed round the island to the boat and Gulliver swam out to it.

He tied the boat to the ships and the sailors towed it slowly back to the shore while Gulliver swam behind it, pushing it along.

When they reached the shore Gulliver pulled the boat on to the beach. With the help of the king's men he got it ready for the voyage home.

Five hundred men made sails for the boat. They quilted together thirteen layers of the strongest material in the kingdom.

Gulliver cut down some tall trees to make a mast and oars and he found a heavy stone to use as an anchor. The boat was soon finished.

He decided to take some tiny cows and sheep home with him. He would have liked to take people as well but the king would not allow it.

At last everything was ready. The king was sad that Gulliver was going and gave him fifty bags of gold coins and a picture of himself as a leaving present. Gulliver put the picture in one of his gloves to keep it safe, then he kissed the king's hand and set sail for home.

Gulliver had only been at sea a few days when, to his excitement, he saw a ship. It was an English ship. Gulliver called and waved.

Luckily the sailors saw him and steered towards the boat. Soon Gulliver was aboard with his tiny animals, feeling very relieved.

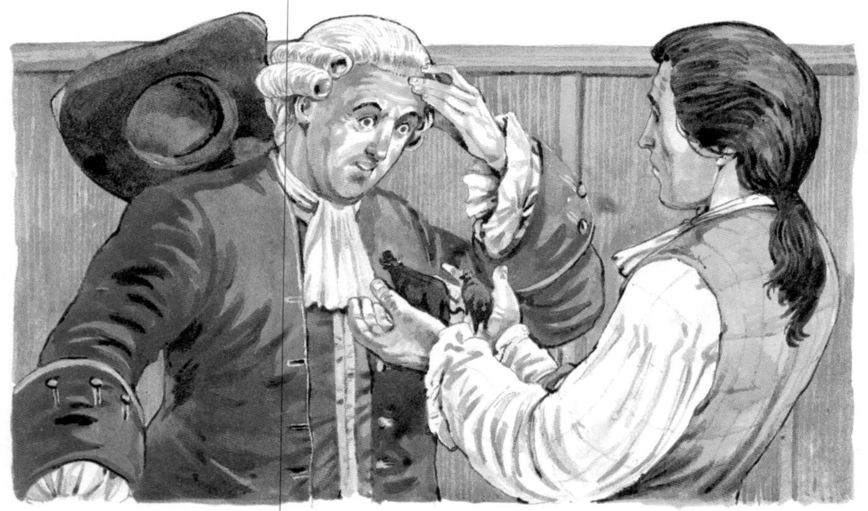

"Welcome," said the captain. "Where have you come from?" Gulliver told him about his adventures on Lilliput and showed him the tiny animals.

The captain was amazed. Gulliver promised him some animals and gold for his voyage home, and they sailed safely back to England.

First published in 1982 by Usborne Publishing Ltd, 20 Garrick Street, London WC2 9BJ, England.

Printed by Casterman S.A.